The New
PLANET

The New
PLANET

CAROLE LOVE FORBES

The New Planet

Copyright © 2022 by Carole Love Forbes. All rights reserved.

No part of this publication may be reproduced, stored in a retrieval system or transmitted in any way by any means, electronic, mechanical, photocopy, recording or otherwise without the prior permission of the author except as provided by USA copyright law.

Published in the United States of America

Library of Congress Control Number: 2022900242
ISBN 978-1-68486-069-2 (Paperback)
ISBN 978-1-68486-070-8 (Digital)

29.11.21

ONE

The crescent moon shone brightly as the sky slowly began its millionth first light of day, on this first day of the first month of the year three thousand two.

People all over the planet were either rising, going to bed, or were functioning somewhere in between. The sun decided to do its usual thing and lift a warming light over the horizon. You experienced the chill in the air, while the weather stations predicted a warm day for the time of the year.

In the living quarters of the Intergalactic Research Society, Alana awoke slowly, opening her eyes with a sense of confusion. She lay still, getting used to the morning light, and treasuring every moment of well-earned rest. Oh, yes. She remembered now; she had worked so late at her research that she had fallen asleep fully dressed on top of her bed. Sometime during the night, she had pulled the fluffy comforter over her.

Her mind was beginning to clear. She quickly checked her watch. "Oh, my goodness, I have fifteen minutes to get to the morning meeting."

She rushed toward her private bathroom, nearly tripping as she quickly shoved her feet into her sandals. "Damn", she muttered.

Exactly twelve minutes later, after a brief shower and a change of clothes, she rushed into the conference room, smoothing her slacks as she headed for her place at the round table. She smiled at her fellow researchers and was rewarded by nods and grunts in reply.

Why was everyone so grouchy? Dr. Townsend, her immediate supervisor and Chief of the Planet Project, was practically growling. He finally spoke.

"As you know, we have been requesting a qualified pilot for over a year now. I made it clear in our requests that this pilot be of high spiritual quality. I received this message this morning from the President, and he is pleased to send us the galaxy's finest space pilot, a Colonel Marc Samson. We all know about his heroic work in the Sisterna Galaxy."

Alana had heard about Colonel Samson, but the things she had gleaned about this famous man, were not all positive. She tried to look pleased, but her heart had sunk at the news.

It was Alana's job to train this new employee, to make him ready for the most sought-after job on the planet. She had hoped for a man with better recommendations, a scientist.

She was startled as the Townsend's voice spoke her name sharply. "I'm sorry, sir. I guess I was thinking ahead. When will Colonel Samson be arriving?"

"He arrived late last night. I wanted to talk to all of you before he joined us." Dr. Townsend replied.

Alana, after many years of working with Townsend, sensed her boss's dissatisfaction with the appointment. Townsend was a master teacher. His enlightenment often blew Alana's mind. Although they had been working closely together for many years, she still felt that she knew more of him from his writings than from personal contact. He was an exceptional man, and he managed not to let his genius deter him from being kind and understanding with his fellow workers. He was still looking at her through his old-fashioned eyeglasses, his pale blue eyes unreadable. He was fairly tall, but thin, and his wrinkled face was graced with a small white beard. He looked away.

"Our work of many years is now at risk. We have been able to reach a plateau where Power One is willing to let us take on the greatest mission our planet has ever attempted. All of this is now totally dependent on a novice to our teachings. We will be facing a horrendous challenge. As well as doing our own projects, we will now have to bring this man to embrace our devotion to this project." Dr. Townsend explained, rubbing his balding head with a shaking hand.

"Do you know why this man was chosen, Doctor?" Dr. Jacob March questioned.

Townsend frowned, pressing his lips together. "The government, thinking in terms of efficiency only, felt they were doing us a great favor by appointing this renowned pilot. However, no matter how much we try to explain, no matter how much we write, they just can't seem to understand that our pilot has to understand our mission, and be totally dedicated to it, as are we. He needs to be able to teach other pilots their jobs, but we must be sure they all understand that spirituality is their primary qualification. How we are to do this in a timely manner is questionable when the teacher does not even have those qualifications."

"How does Samson feel about this appointment, Doctor?" Alana piped in.

"I haven't had time to interview him, so I invited him to join us here. Time is of the essence. We will have to decide at this meeting. There is no doubt that he will be completely ignorant of our work. The thing we must decide is whether we can accept this man. We need to know today if he is willing to be trained to the position," Dr. Townsend explained

"Alana, it is vital that you take in everything about this man, as it will be your job to indoctrinate him into our state of consciousness. I have great confidence in you, my dear, and I am eager to hear your opinion of Samson." "Since I am on the same page with you, Doctor, you can count on me to delve deeply into his consciousness and determine what type of man he is," Alana promised.

One of the society's clerks knocked on the tall wooden doors and announced the arrival of the main subject of the morning, Colonel Marc Samson.

As a tall, good looking man in his late thirties, dressed in military uniform, stepped into the doorway.

As much as Alana was aware that first impressions were very often not to be trusted, she had an immediate feeling of disappointment, as she noticed the young man's obvious impersonal attitude, and sensed his egotism. So many years of being around teachers, masters and enlightened scientists had made her forget the negative impact of an overactive, slightly negative, personality. She watched Samson intently as Townsend introduced him to the board, which consisted, in addition to herself, Dr. Henderson and Dr. March, PHD Olivia Blake, three other men, and another woman.

She was surprised that the Colonel was so young. Though she knew him to be around thirty, he looked more like he was in his early 20's. He had an athlete's body which seemed to give off its own energy. His face was square, with a strong jawline. His nose was slightly curved above a wide mouth, and his eyes, like his hair, were brown, though his eyes were flecked with gold. Alana scolded herself for having noticed that.

Dr. Edwin Smyth was their geo-physicist, and was in charge of the designing and building of the new spaceships for the planet project. He was short and round in the middle. Time had reduced the hair on his head to a few wisps above his ears, which, surprisingly managed to hold up very thick spectacles. Dr. James Campion was the spiritual leader of the project, and Olivia Blake oversaw suiting and equipment.

The group greeted Samson with smiles and handshakes, but Alana held back, merely smiling at him across the conference table. Henderson, noticing her reticence, called her over and introduced her to Samson.

"This is as our head coordinator on this gigantic project, Dr. Alana Hargate." Samson flashed her a wide smile and reached for her hand. "Glad to meet you, Miss Hargate."

Alana pulled her hand away gently, her smile never reaching her eyes. "It is Doctor Hargate, Colonel. We will be working very closely. I will expect you at my office at 0800 tomorrow."

Samson was surprised by her coolness but impressed by her appearance. She was so much younger than he had imagined when told about her and the project. She was slim, about five foot six, with dark hair paged softly around her oval face. Her features were even, a small straight nose, and full lips. Most attractive were her large, heavily lashed turquoise eyes. He wanted to access her figure, but this was neither the time nor the place.

After all the introductions were made and each doctor welcomed Samson, Townsend released his people, and settled into questions

Samson. Alana so wanted to sit in on this interview but accepted the protocol. She knew that Henderson would brief her later.

As Alana walked down the long hall toward her office, she wondered if she was up to the enormous task facing her. She knew the rules. She had studied for many months before she had the process computed. She had read and reread every paper she could on the process and had researched it on the master computer.

The project was something that the planet's top minds had been working toward for hundreds of years. They had finally been given the go ahead over a year ago, but it had taken this long to find the right pilot to bring the project into reality.

She brushed a tendril of raven hair back from her forehead, as she stopped at the door of her office. She stood there for a moment experiencing an extremely rare moment of self-doubt. Then she pulled back her shoulders, lifted her chin, and entered her well-ordered office.

She must not judge this man so quickly. His manner might just be covering up an exceptional spirit. She would wait. She would work with him every day. Like all living creatures, he was a spiritual entity in a human body. Though he appeared to be unaware of that fact, it was her job to bring him to an active awareness of this if he were to prove useful to the project. In this she would be helped by Dr. Campion. He was so extraordinary in his faith that she took advantage of every moment she could spend with him.

"I know what I need," she sighed. She approached a comfortably soft padded chair near the window. She sat down and gazed out at the expansive park which was part of the Society. As she took in the beauty of the trees and flowering plants, she felt herself relax. She closed her eyes and let herself slip into a meditative state.

After so many years of meditation, she effortlessly went into the deepest part of her, and let herself be open to communication with her highest self. Soon pictures began to appear before her closed eyes, and as they became more clearly defined, she saw Samson's face before her. He did not speak, but he reached out and touched her cheek. He smiled at her, and she watched, fascinated, as his uniform disappeared. He was now dressed in white robes.

She was suddenly filled with a wonderful warm feeling of confidence. She watched until the picture of Samson slowly faded away, and then brought herself slowly back into alert consciousness.

"Thank you." she smiled, and feeling free and energetic, rose and went to her desk to again review the first steps in Samson's training. As she opened her manual, she found a small picture of Samson. He had a warm smile on his face. Alana smiled to herself. "This might not be so bad after all."

Samson had been given twenty-four hours to unpack and get his small apartment in order.

He was pleased that he had a homey apartment rather than a cold room. He tried to push away his feelings that he was a fish out of water, but they clung to him. He wished he could have refused this appointment, but duty, as usual, called.

He spent the day trying to make himself feel at home. He unpacked a few of his books and read a while. He was hungry but did not know where to find food. His frig was empty.

Promptly at six o'clock a young man knocked on Marc's door. When he told Marc that he could either go to the dining room for dinner or have his dinner brought to him, he quickly checked the menu the young man gave him and picked out steak, mashed potatoes and green beans, to be brought to his apartment.

"Do you have anything to drink? Marc asked.

"Oh, sorry Colonel, we don't handle that, but you have a liquor cabinet in your parlor. I'll show you where it is."

"That is alright, young man. I'll find it."

As Terry had promised a hot a delicious dinner arrived a half hour later and everything was delicious. The steak was medium rare and tender. With a full tummy and a glass of Merlot, Marc finally managed to relax.

He was awakened at six a.m. by the same young man, who offered to show him to the dining room for breakfast. While on their way to the dining room, the young man explained a few of the activities they saw as they walked. Marc finally realized that the young man must be assigned to him, so he asked for his name and was told it was Terry.

THE NEW PLANET

Terry gave him a big smile. "This is a mighty big place, but I will show you all of the places you need to know. Also, if you will give me a grocery list, I will see your cabinets and frig are full."

Marc thanked Terry. He found he liked the lad. After a breakfast of Danish Waffles, bacon, and two cups of black coffee, Marc let Terry show him to Doctor Hargate's office.

Alana arose early after a good night's sleep. She dressed comfortably, had a good breakfast in the smaller cafeteria, then headed toward her office. Samson was waiting at her door, leaning against the wall.

"Good morning, teach. You look beautiful."

Ignoring his comment, she opened the door, and gestured him in. However, he surprised her by stopping her from entering the office. "Look, teach. I am a man of space. This whole complex is giving me claustrophobia. Can we just take a ride or something before we get started? "Well," she stammered. "We don't really have time for that. There is so much to cover today, and we are so far behind our original schedule."

"I understand, but you can talk to me, explain what is going on here, while we ride, can't you?"

She thought for a moment, and then decided. "A ride would take too long and would take your focus off what I have to relate to you. But…we could walk in the Society's parkland behind the complex. It is a beautiful day, and we could work there until lunch." "Fantastic. Let's go, lady." She let the office door swing closed, and then he took her arm and draped it over his. Show the way, Teach." She flinched at the nickname but forced herself to let it pass.

After traversing several hallways and descending to the basement floor in the elevator, they reached a heavy door which opened out onto the parkland.

It was a beautiful day. The sun was shining brightly, but it was not hot. There was a freshening breeze which felt good on their faces. They strolled to the area where there was a small, landscaped lake and tables and stools to sit on.

The air was filled with the soothing sounds of beautiful, melodic music.

"Where's the music coming from?" Samson asked.

"We have it piped in all over the complex. We find it very soothing."

"It's not bad. I guess I'll get used to it." Samson smiled.

Alana led him to a bench close to the shore of a small lake, and they sat, enjoying their surroundings. There were several types of ducks and a swan family floating leisurely on the water. "It's odd, but I don't come out here often enough. It is so refreshing. There is something about nature that touches your inner being and makes you feel exceptionally alive and well." Alana sighed.

"I'm an outdoor man, myself." Samson smiled. "If you think this is great, you should let me take you up on a space flight. There is nothing like it. Makes you feel like you own the world. But I promised you we would work. I'm at a total loss as to why I am here, and why the President chose me."

"I can understand that, and we will be spending the next few months trying to help you understand our mission, and where you fit into it."

"Will I still be flying? I don't think I could stand being grounded."

"You will eventually be flying a lot and teaching other pilots. It is vital that we know which galaxies you are familiar with and how many more universes you have traveled to."

"I have flown to many other planets like this one. However, I was born on a much smaller planet than this named Sisterna. I realized my love of flying at a very young age and worked very hard at many types of jobs until I had enough money to go to Space College."

He reached down and picked up a small stick with which he drew patterns on the damp earth. "I heard you speak about spirituality at the meeting, and I know that this planet has reached a high level of spirituality, and an even higher level of enlightenment. I must confess, I think the committee might have sent you the wrong man. I am not a very spiritual person. I am just an ordinary guy who likes to fly the universes. I must admit though that I do sometimes wonder what makes the universes function, and what the heck my part in it is."

Alana was pleased to hear that Samson had a sense that there might be something in him that he had never thought much about.

Alana smiled. "We have come a long way. Our planetary history is one of duality, godlessness, greed and violence. Through our first few centuries, we had lost hope that we would ever learn to love and appreciate each other, and that we would come to know who we really are. We had lost track of our oneness." "Yes. I was forced to study planetary history in college. How is it that this planet has changed so drastically? It doesn't seem possible that such peace and prosperity could have evolved out of a world so at war with itself."

"According to the Society's records, the change came about quite suddenly in our twenty-first century. The world seemed to be falling apart. Governments were being exposed for their greed and lack of caring for the population. There were terrorist attacks and riots. On top of all that horror, Mother Nature was attacking us on every level. The population was in despair.

Then, with the help of our guardians and Power One, there began a massive change of consciousness. Through mass media, people in countries all over the world began to communicate with each other, and to discover that their likenesses greatly outnumbered their differences.

People began to appreciate each other. They began to love themselves and that opened them up to the awareness of the people around them and were now able to love each other more. They started caring about the animal populations that had survived extinction, and put their efforts into providing them care and safety.

It came about slowly, and during all the fear, but in the context of man-made time, it was lightning fast."

"And your people are all perfect now?" he queried. "No, not perfect, but working at it. At least we have learned to love and help one another and have come a long way toward eliminating fear. We finally know who we are, and that we are all one. We can now give more time and love to our personal and mutual missions rather than doubting ourselves and our creator. But this is not my responsibility for this mission. I am here to indoctrinate you, and help you understand the changes which will be taking place in your life and your thinking. You will have several guides and teachers to help you in the areas in which the mission will utilize your skills."

"So, when will I be told what our mission is?"

Alana checked her watch. "That is your first lesson, Colonel. The master teachers have long known of a project that only the highest spiritually populated and educated planets can be awarded."

She rose from her seat and moved toward the lake, where she stood for a moment gathering her thoughts. "As you are aware, the universes that we have been able to travel to are just a handful of the many universes out there." She gestured toward the sky with her arm.

"We have been given records of past activities in this area. It has been made clear to us at the Society that each planet which has reached a high enough level of spirituality has the privilege and the rare opportunity to replant life on a new planet that will support our type of living creatures." "A new planet? But where would it be?" Samson asked as he rose and came to her side.

"We have been shown one in a universe millions of light years away from ours.

But you will learn all about this during your training period. I can tell you where you will fit into this mission, and what you will be called upon to do. That is if you are ready to hear it." Alana looked up and into his eyes. She welcomed the look of willingness and eagerness she found there.

"This new little planet has existed for many ages, but it still in its infancy," she continued. "It boasts two great oceans, which makes it an excellent choice for planting life."

"You are going to put people on this planet?"

"Eventually, but the development and advancement of this planet has to be timed perfectly. You see, from our perspective, the movements of this new planet are speeded up, so that many hundreds of years can take place there, when only months will pass here."

"How will you get this planet populated?"

"All of this information will be given to you by several masters in all of the areas in which your talents will be needed. I will be your go between, and see that you get the best training available"

"But...where do I fit in?" He frowned.

"I will give you a short outline which your teachers will fill in. When the new planet has reached a point in its development where we can introduce our level of life, a master teacher will need to plant the seeds, and watch over them during its growth. You and your trainees will be called upon to transport the spiritual masters who will be doing the planting, and education of the spirits destined to populate this planet." Marc took a deep breath. "Wow!" "But we have been out here long enough. You must have lunch now, and then you will have the afternoon off to contemplate what you have learned this morning."

Alana started to walk toward the path to the research building, and then stopped to wait for Samson, who was still standing near the lake, scratching his head.

"Come. You'll feel better when you have something in your stomach." She laughed and held out her hand to Samson, who shook his head and moved to take her hand.

"Wow! I suspected it would be something big, but a new planet. There sure must be something to this spirituality stuff." They walked back down the path to the building. Marc was still holding her hand. It made her feel a little uncomfortable, so she gently pulled her hand away and covered her movement by pushing the habitually wayward lock of hair off of her forehead. Marc just smiled.

Alana had spent her free time after dinner re-reading the file on Marc Samson. She could not help but feel that the information in Marc's file was rather superficial. Even at this extremely short contact with the Colonel, she sensed a hidden depth. It would be her job to bring these secret thoughts and feelings to the fore. It was the only way he would be able to succeed in his appointed job with the Society.
Alana was up early this morning, anxious to get started with the Colonel. She headed away from the residential apartments, and down a long hall until she reached the cafeteria. She took a seat at a table near the window and looked around the room. Samson was not

there, so she figured he had slept late. This was not a good sign, but she ate her breakfast of eggs and fruit, and started out of the cafeteria.

Before she had taken ten steps, a smiling Marc Samson stood before her.

"I thought you were going to sleep all day, teach." "Have you had your breakfast?" Alana asked.

"Oh, hours ago. I always get up at 4:30 every morning and so some running and some warm-ups."

Alana's eyes took in the space suit that Samson was wearing. "Do you always exercise in a space suit?"

Samson laughed. "Hardly ever, teach, but today is a very special day." Alana frowned.

I guess Dr. Henderson did not tell you. As you know, for the last five years I have been employed by a company on my planet, Sisterna, to pick up and deliver items from there and from sister planets and deliver them to other planets."

"Yes, that is what you used to do. You won't need a spacesuit in our research for many months." Alana explained.

"Well, the Society arranged for me to do one last job which I was signed for. I have my last mission on spaceship, Horizon, today."

"Oh, well, I guess we can get started when you return. How many days will this mission take?" Alana asked.

"Oh, I will be back late this afternoon."

"Then I will meet you here tomorrow morning at eight thirty." She started to turn away, but Samson took her arm. She looked up at him questioningly.

"I was hoping you would like to go with me." He smiled.

She was taken aback, even a little shocked at this invitation. "You want me to go up in space?"

"If you haven't been up before this, this is an opportunity you should not miss."

"I have hardly left the Society since I graduated and got my masters at the University of Space. The thought of going out into space has never entered my mind."

"I had a suit delivered to your room. When you are ready, meet me at the space dock."

"But what makes you think I will go with you?"

"You, my fine teacher, are a scientist. You will not be able to resist seeing what is taking place in other galaxies. On top of that, what you will see and hear today will probably fit right into your Society's project. Ten minutes!"

"There is no way I can get myself into a space suit in ten minutes," she complained.

The man who delivered your suit will assist you. And you may want to take a journal. This will be an unforgettable day for you."

Samson smiled and walked down a hall which would eventually take him to the space port. Alana watched him, shaking her head in disbelief. Had she really agreed to his offer? She took a deep breath and nodded her head. "Yes, you ninny, you did."

Alana did not make it to the space dock in ten minutes. It was more like twenty-five, but Samson didn't complain. "You look cute in a space suit," he smiled.

"I feel like a mummy. These things weigh a ton." she complained. He handed her a large helmet with a glass front. "Do I have to wear one of these things?"

"Until the ship gets to a certain speed, then the air and temperature will be monitored by the ship's computers. These smaller transport jets aren't as up-to-date as the tremendous galaxy ships that carry large crews on active duty for years at a time, but she will get us where we are going."

Alana started to don her space helmet but was having trouble with it. She jumped when she heard a female voice coming up behind her.

"Here, let me help you with that." Alana turned as she recognized the voice.

"Olivia, what are you doing here?"

"I was working on a design in the chart room when I heard Dr. Henderson say that you were going to go up with the Colonel today. Thought I might give you some moral support."

Alana smiled. She was relieved to see a familiar face in the docking area. Olivia was a good friend and having another woman in the same unit made workdays easier. Alana smiled. "Good, you are here. Help me with this monster, please."

"Oh, you silly goose you do not need this particular monster for where you are going today." Alana looked at Olivia. "Do you know where we are going? Olivia smiled. "No honey, your colonel has kept that quite secret. But I know it will be quite an adventure." Samson joined them, smiling. "Let's go. We do not have all day." He took Alana's arm and helped her into the ship. Alana turned and said goodbye to Olivia who stood there wearing a big smile.

Alana would not admit, even to herself that she was a bit frightened, so she came up with a wide smile. "You are sure we will be coming back." Samson showed her to a seat next to where he would be flying the ship. "We are going to a special place that only a few people know it exists."

"What? That sounds impossible in these times." Alana replied.

"It is extremely important in this case due to protecting what lives on this spot." Alana was hooked now. "Oh, Marc. How fascinating. Let's get going. I can hardly wait." Samson then went through several interesting moves until the motors roared and the ship shook. Alana took a deep breath. "It is all right, my dear. I know exactly what I am doing. Here we go." Alana forced a wide smile. "Up, up and away!"

The world around them changed and the views of objects in the sky became less crowded. Exactly one hour later the conversation came to a halt. "I want you to watch closely now for something coming into view on our left." Marc advised.

"Oh, are we there?" Marc smiled "Almost." "But I do not see anything."

"That is the way it is supposed to be." Alana turned to him. "What do you mean?" Marc turned off a few buttons. "This planet is a secret. I am letting you into this secret because I have found you to be trustworthy and also because it involves you."

"Me? How can that be?" "That is something you will learn today." "What do you mean?" Alana blurted.

THE NEW PLANET

"Look! Can you see those thin colored lines? Over to your left. See the lines appearing?"

Alana searched the sky, finding nothing. "The fact that the surroundings of this planet are thickly hidden assures its safety." Alana queried, "But what could make this planet so important?" "You will see shortly." Marc assured. And the next few minutes provided many colors surrounding the ship as it made its way toward a landing field on the planet. Soon Alana spied a landing field and held on tight as the ship came safely to the ground.

"Oh, this is unbelievable!" Alana cried out. "How wonderful!" The next half hour was spent cooling down the motors and watching for someone to meet them. Suddenly a bright white light appeared near the front of the ship. Alana watched closely as the light moved toward the doors. "Oh, my God. What is that?" "That is our host. Keep watching and you will see."

Alana watched as the light came into the ship and came close to her. She let out a little yelp as her body was surrounded in warmth and a deep spiritual blessing.

"What is it, Marc?" Marc smiled. "Not what. Who?" Marc put his arm around a trembling Alana. As Alana watched, the bright light dimmed, and an aging man appeared in its place. Alana sucked in a deep breath. "Oh!" Marc smiled. "I would like to introduce you to our host, Father Francis Campion." I took a few minutes for Alana to reply while she stared at an elderly man who looked like he was in his hundreds. He had long white hair hanging over his shoulders and a long beard to match it covering a smiling face. "Welcome, my dear. I have been anxious to see you and take care of our business."

"Business?" Alana asked. "I am a little confused." She turned to Marc. "Is this supposed to be a surprise?" Mark looked a little ashamed. "Sorry, Alana. I thought you would understand when we got here and met this great spiritual leader. Father Campion oversees this wonderful planet which has a fantastically important job."

"Job, what kind of job?" Alan questions Campion. He smiles, "Why do we not got to our main building where we can get something in our stomachs and get acquainted."

Marc moved to Alana and took her arm. "Come on, beautiful, let us find out why we are here." Alana gave him a smart look. "I think that is a very good idea, sir."

The reverent left Alana and Marc at a long table filled with delicious looking food and excused himself. Alana and Marc filled up on as much as they could swallow and sat back in their comfortable chairs.

"I wonder where he went?" Alana questioned. Marc thought it was about time to fill her in. "My dear, do you have any idea who this man is and why we are here?" "I know it is a lot more than a little vacation trip. I would appreciate your filling me in. Where are we and why are we really here?"

"I really am sorry. I wanted you to enjoy the ride, so I kept my mouth shut. But I may have been wrong. I really do not know much about why you are here, but he goes. Dr. Smyth had me bring you here for a meeting with Father Campion. I do not know what it is all about but here we are."

Their conversation was halted by a young man in robes. He spoke to Alana and asked her to follow him to speak with Father Campion. Alana looked to Marc for support, but he smiled and squeezed her hand. "It will be fine, honey…woops…Alana." Alana smiled and took the hand of the young man and they went to the back of the huge room where they went through a heavy set of beautiful drapes and into a rather dark room where a warming fireplace filled a whole side of the room. Before the fireplace Father Campion sat on a tall white decorative chair. He started to rise but Alana waved him back in his chair.

"I am so honored to speak with you, Father. How can I be of service to you?" "My dear, you will soon discover that you will be of service to thousands." "Thousands of people, sir?" "Not people, child. Animals." Alana was at a loss. "Animals sir?"

"Are you not an animal lover?" Alana was embarrassed. "Why I have not been around too many animals. I only recently met some of them, and I was impressed by them." Father Campion shook his head. "Why I thought you would be a great animal lover, but I trust Dr. Townsend's opinion and welcome you to Restorium."

THE NEW PLANET

"Restorium. That is an interesting name for a planet." "Yes, and it makes this planet the perfect place for those who were not able to live a good life on their native planet."

"I do not quite understand, Father." He smiled. "Then shame on Townsend. I think it is time for me to explain the reason for your being here. Sit down, my child."

Alana slipped onto a huge pillow at the feet of Father Campion and took a deep breath.

"I hear that you have been working on the birth of our new planet, and doing spectacular work, and I have decided that you will be the best person to take care of my children."

Alana perked up. "Your children?" Campion smiled. "Yes, and there are millions of them." Alana's jaw dropped. "Millions?" "Yes, child. You see, my children are all the animals of the many universes."

"Amazing. Animals! How can they be your children?" "We think of children as those who we must care for and protect. My animal friends are much in need of love and protection. Life in the places where the animals thrive have been taken over by the selfish needs of man so they cannot survive. We here at Restorium provide the animals who have lost their homes with homes which provide them with all they need to live, have children, and be happy until we can provide them with safe homes on other planets."

"How wonderful!" Alana sighed. "Yes, this is a wonderful place, and we have many great animals living here in nice places. If you want to, I will take you around today to see some of them." Alana smiled. "Yes, I would love to see them. I have never seen any wild animals."

"My dear, there are no 'wild' animals, only animals working at staying alive and continuing their species. You will see how wonderful they all are. But those clothes are too uncomfortable for traveling around." He motioned to a young man who had entered the room. "Michael, please take or guest and get her clothed in something cool." The young man led Alana out of the room. Father Campion went into deep meditation and came out of it smiling.

A half hour later Alana was again with Father Campion as they came upon a small train-like track and got into a decorated engine.

They got comfortable and Campion started it moving forward. As they moved through the countryside Alana was surprised how the country around them changed to different types of landscapes. Finally, the engine stopped, and the country was that of the Savanna, with Umbrella Thorne Acacia trees and river bushwillow grew in the plains.

Surprisingly, an extremely tall animal moved out into their sight. Alana was shocked. "Oh my!" "What is that?" "That, my dear, is a Giraffe. They live in the Savanna of Africa. They eat from the trees. Are they not magnificent?" Alana was impressed. "It is hard to believe that anything built like that would be able to survive." Campion smiled. "They do fine as long man does not butt in. So, we take the survivors in and keep them until a better planet comes along."

As they moved on, Alana learned about many animals who were housed on Restorium.

When the little mover brought them back to the starting place, Alana turned to Father Campion, a look of loss on her face. "I can see, Father, that you are doing wonderful work for these animals, but that still does not explain why I am here." Campion smiled. "Yes, you are right. Come with me to a spot near the waterfall and I will tell you how important you are to all of these animals."

When they were seated on soft pillows near the waterfall, Father Campion spoke, "It is obvious we need someone to see that animals will need to be entered onto the new planet we are birthing. The question now is should they be put on the planet fully activated or should we put their DNA on first. Would you consider talking about this problem?" Alana was quiet for a while, then sighed. "Well, the major problem I can see is how little I know these animals. You know everything so how could we successfully come to any kind of agreement?"

Campion looked into her eyes and found what he wanted to find. "You care, my dear. That is what counts. I watched you as you were introduced to these fine creatures and I could feel the love in your heart. Love is major and you have it. We will sit in the prayer room and pray over this to come to some answers as to how to get animals safely to this new planet and provide safe homes for them. But now my dear, I am going to take you through the waterfall and be blessed by its cool sprays."

While this meeting was going on Marc asked if he could see some of the animals. Given a hearty yes, he settled into the little motor train and set off. He loved animals, wild or pets, so it was a great visit for him. His favorites were the lions. Their beauty filled his heart with joy, but most impressive to him were how the lions had families and would sit beneath trees and enjoy all being together. Of course, the mama lions had to carefully watch over their babies to protect them from the males. He sat and watched a family for a long time, then went on to enjoy the other animals. After he had seen all that he wanted to he walked back to the main house and was treated to a big slice of cake. Getting a little worried as to where Alana was, he walked out to the animal track and found it empty. Just as he was turning to go back to the main house, he turned and saw something moving in the closest waterfall. Then he saw Father Campion come out from behind the waterfall. Alana soon followed the Father and Marc decided he would watch and see what they were going to do. He scratched his head, wondering what the two totally different types of people were doing for such a long time. The Father was used to being kept in his private places and not let people wear him out.

Marc was amazed. In all the times he had visited Restorium he had never seen anyone be within a few feet of the Father. As he watched Father Campion stopped in front of the splashing waterfall and looked up. Alana also looked up and it was obvious they were now in prayer.

Then the Father turned and walk right into the rushing water of the falls. Alana did not hesitate. She moved quickly into the rushing water to his side.

Marc watched this with bated breath. He moved slowly toward the falls, his mind full of questions. Was Alana more than the lovely woman he was learning to care for? What was it about this woman? What about her made Father Francis honor her so? Just as he reached the falls Father Campion and Alana appeared at his side.

Father Francis smiled at Marc. "Thank you my son. You have fulfilled a promise made to me the first time you found the way onto this planet." Marc's brows tightened as he tried to remember such a promise. Francis smiled at him. "Don't waste your time, you made your promise through your Christ self. All you need to know now is that a great moment of enlightenment has taken place and that we have all been blessed by it. Now we will have some light refreshment and then we will get started on our trip.

By the time the lunch was over both Alana and Marc were feeling like themselves again.

Father Francis led them through the forest to a landing field where a small vehicle awaited them. "I will see you when you return, young ones, enjoy your trip". Father Francis departed, leaving the two sitting in the small vehicle.

Alana looked at Marc questioningly. "You still haven't told me what we are doing here."

"Sorry, I wanted all of this to be a surprise for you, but it is time to tell you what you are going to see."

"Definitely" she said as she poked him in his ribs. He laughed. "Also, I had to know how you feel about animals."

"Animals?"

"Yes. I know you worked and lived in a place that did not have time to think about animals, but what I saw at Aunt Ellies house made me see the loving side of you and your kindness toward our greatest gift from Power-One which is animals."

"So, this is all about animals. What kind of animals and what makes them so important that a great teacher like Father Francis would be interested in them?"

"I will explain as we go along. We only have a short time to spend here so let us get going." With that Marc pressed a couple of buttons and the small vehicle pulled away, heading along a path that seemed to lead somewhere. But there was nothing on either side of the vehicle to see. After a few minutes of no sounds and no visuals Alana looked sideways at Marc.

"What the heck is going on? There is nothing here to see."

"Be patient, we are almost to the first stop."

THE NEW PLANET

"First stop? How many stops are there?" "Wait and see. We won't spend much time at each stop, but you will find all of the stops worth waiting for."

A couple minutes later, Marc hit a button and the vehicle pulled to a stop. He punched another button and the vast savannas appeared on both sides of the vehicle. Alana's breath caught.

"Oh, Marc. This is fantastic." That earned her a big smile. As they moved through the savanna Marc was tickled at all of the oohs and aahs loudly expressed by his passengers. There were many small and even a few handsome lions moving about.

Suddenly as they saw a huge tree from which loud growling sounds rang out. As Alana screamed, Oh Marc, do something! If they see us, they might attack." Marc put his hand on her arm to comfort her. No problem lady. They cannot get through the invisible walls to harm us. In fact, they do not even know we are here."

"How can that be? They are right next to us." "There is a barrier high over them and between them and us."

But I do not see any barrier."

"What it is made of and how it works are known only to Father Francis. This barrier is totally impenetrable. However, no animal would attack us anyway as they cannot see us."

"That is fantastic. They can live in peace with no men with guns to kill them."

"Yes, it protects them, but no one who is not accepted by Father Francis would ever be allowed on this train, anyway, are you ready to continue?"

"I would like to see it all."

"I guess I have not made it clear. This is not a zoo. It is a planetarium. The whole of planet Restorium is for animals, plants, birds and all living creatures. Here they live in safety and Privacy, doing the things they naturally do, with no humans getting in their way."

"But what if an animal is injured. How do veterinarians get in there to aid them?"

"They have been promised a natural life here with no intervention."

"Seems cruel in a way, but I can see if would be best for them. But where did they come from and why is there a whole planet for them to share?"

"I am afraid I do not have all the facts, lady. Can you not just watch them and appreciate their beauty and majesty?"

"I would be ever so grateful if you would stop calling me 'lady'. I have a name", she frowned.

"Oh, of course. Alana, isn't it? Beautiful name. Sorry. And you can call me Marc."

"Okay." Alana smiled and looked back at the animals as they slowly drove past. "They Are so much more wonderful than the pictures of them. Can we see some others?"

She looked back at the plane and let out a loud gasp.

"Oh my God. Stop! Can you stop this cart? I do not believe what I am seeing. Mark followed her gaze and laughed. "it is…Alana.

Dinosaurs, at least two different types. How is that for animal size and strength?"

"But this is pronominal! Living dinosaurs! But how can this be?"

"I told you that all of the animal species are domiciled on this planet. That means all."

Marc started the tram and Alana sat in thought as they headed back to the compound. Marc brought her out of her trance with a warm smile.

"Well, we have time to see some elephants if they are near the track. They are usually on the move. I know Father Francis wants to spend some time with you and then we have to be on our way back to the institute."

Marc pushed a couple of buttons and the tram shot ahead. As they went, they passed many other animals that were comfortable on the savanna. But Alana's favorite of all the animals they saw was one infant elephant who was playing in a small puddle of mud while its mama was dipping into the deeper water of a stream. Alana laughed until her tummy ached. Marc was surprised to see that side of her. She was always so serious. When she finally looked up at him, her face flushed and happy, he was pleased to note her true beauty.

"Oh, Marc, they are all so wonderful. I love them all. It would be pretty hard to take them all to the institute though," she laughed.

"I wish we could stay longer, but we should have been on our way back a half hour ago. I do not want to stand Father Francis up." He let out a yip. "Hold onto your hat, here we go."

Marc pulled a cord and their seats swung around to face the opposite direction. They were on their way back. Alana watched the animals for a while as they sped by, then she sat back and, after a deep breath, she relaxed and finally dozed.

When she awoke they were pulling into the dock. A servant helped them debark and when they reached the clearing where they were to meet their host, they found a delicious light salad for lunch. A few minutes later Father Francis joined them. Alana smiled at him.

"Thank you so much for letting me see those wonderful animals. It made me remember the smaller animals that were on Planet Venachius where I was born. I had forgotten how much I loved them. But I am amazed. There were animals there that have been extinct on our planet for centuries."

Father Francis smiled. "Has it not occurred to you, my dear, that this planet is the sanctuary for all animals that can no longer exist on their home planet. When there is a place for them their DNA is shipped to their new home. This way we have a home for them, and healthy bodies to enjoy." Alana could not talk for a moment, then she smiled. "I am so happy for them, Father Francis."

"And I am pleased, my child. Now, if you have finished your afternoon snack, I would appreciate a short time with you before you have to leave."

"Of course, Father Francis. It will be my pleasure." As they walked into the forest, Marc again wondered about the attention paid to Alana by an extremely important man. When Dr. Townsend had given him the day off and suggested he might take Alana out for some free time, he had thought it was a little strange, but he knew Alana needed to get out of her office and see what the outside world was like.

A half hour later Father Francis and Alana returned. Alana looked like she was in a daze, but she followed Marc to his ship. It did not take Marc long to have them on their way. Alana was surprisingly mute. She acted like she was in some sort of trance. He gave orders to the computer to takeoff and then they headed for home. Then he took her hand and led her to a comfortable couch. He helped her and then sat down with her.

"Alana are you, all right?" She did not answer, so he shook her gently by her shoulders. "Please talk to me, Alana. What happened? What is the matter?"

She finally looked at him and to his shock, she snapped at him.

"How could you do this to me? I thought we were beginning to be friends. Friends can be trusted."

"I do not understand. What are you talking about?" He urged.

"I thought you took me to Restorium for a day of vacation. Why did you not tell me?"

"I wanted to give you a day of fun. What are you talking about?"

"You knew what they had planned, did you not? How could you let me walk right into that?"

"Lady, I do not know what you are talking about."

"Oh, sure. You did not know what it was all about," Alana snapped.

"No. I still do not know what you are talking about." Marc turned around in his chair to face Alana. "Now start at the beginning. What is it that you think I have done?"

"Oh, just fly your machine and leave me alone!" Alana crossed her arms over her chest and turned her face away from Marc.

"No, no, lady. None of that. Look at me and tell me what I am supposed to be guilty of."

Alana sat silent for a while, but Marc did not back off. He stared at her hard until she finally relented. "You are claiming that you did not know what Father Francis revealed to me, right?"

"I am as innocent as a babe, can you tell me, or is a secret?"

All right. I will give you the benefit of a doubt. Oh, I just cannot believe it. How could this have happened?

"Go on," Marc prodded.

"I have been a loyal employer at the institute since I was eighteen. I thought I was appreciated and trusted."

THE NEW PLANET

"And what Father Francis told you, you are not sure anymore?" Marc probed.

"According to the Father I am no longer in charge of the new employees,"

"Did he give you a reason?"

"He claimed the move is an honor. He said I should be proud."

"That does not sound too bad. Did he say what your new job would be?"

"He certainly did. Me of all people. Why would they decide to give this job to me? What on earth would make them think I could do it? I am an expert on men and women, but animals? What the hell do I know about animals?"

"Wait a minute. you are going to work with animals?"

"They have put me in charge of planting all of the animals on the new planet. Me!"

"Wait a minute, you are going to work with animals?"

Marc was silent for a moment, lost in thought. Then his eyes popped, and he grabbed Alana's hand in his.

"Woman, are you mad? That is a fantastic opportunity. They have honored you beyond belief. And your wages are going to explode. I am so happy for you."

"Happy. You know how much I know about animals. I cannot do this."

"Yes, you can, and you will."

"But why me?"

"I think I can give you an answer to that, Alana. It is obvious they have been watching you for a long time. They know what a loving, giving person you are. And seeing you with the animals in my aunt's house shows me you will fall in love with all of animals as you study them."

Alana threw her arms up. "Oh, dear Power One! I am going back to school! How could this be happening?"

"Look at it this way. You were the one who was so excited to have the opportunity to being part of building a new planet. Well, now you are a more important part. You can now choose which animals could survive on the new planet, and what animals could survive in each type of weather in each environment. Open your eyes, lady. You are headed into a whole new, exciting life."

Alana sat back in her seat and took a deep breath. "So, you really feel I can do it, Marc?"

"I know you can. Let's get this ship moving. We should be able to get home in time for dinner. I am going to take you to the fanciest eating establishment we can find outside the institute." The smile on her face set his heart to pumping. She might not be so bad after all.

TWO

Tired but happy Alana opened the door to her small room and moved to put down her things. Suddenly she felt something soft and warm move across her legs. She jumped and let out a yelp. Looking down she saw something so unbelievable that she dropped everything and jumped back. She stood there for a few moments gazing down at the small creature who was looking up at her with round eyes.

She took another deep breath. Was she crazy or was a small pink piglet staring up at her and wiggling its small body as if it were dancing?

She went down on her knees and touched the squiggly little creature.

"What on earth are you doing here, little one? Are you the same little pig that I met at Aunt Ellie's house?" The piglet gave her an answering wiggle. "But what are you doing here, piglet?" As she gave her visitor a pet, she saw a small note attached to a red velvet collar. She unfolded the note and read. "My dear Alana, I figured you have been alone long too long, so here is my fine piglet to keep you company. You can name him what you wish as we just called him piggy," It was signed Aunt Ellie.

As Alana looked down at the small animal who apparently was now hers, she felt a lump form in her throat. She picked the piglet up and held him close to her heart.

"I am thrilled to have you in my life. I love you already and I know that love will grow as we share lives together. I cannot see any fluffy name for you, so I am going to call you Maxwell."

As the weeks flew by Alana prized her little friend more and more as she found her free time filled with laughs and hugs.

Dr. Smyth shook his bespectacled head. As usual he was deep into his profoundly creative mind. Marc Samson sat in silence waiting for his teacher to settle on a thought that he could put into words. After a silence of fifteen minutes, Samson moved slightly in his chair knowing that that tiny movement would bring Dr. Smyth back into the room.

Smyth was the youngest of the famous scientists at the society. However, his job was the most difficult, but intriguing, project of the teams. When Marc had finally been tuned into his own place in this project, he had been amazed and a little, no, a lot, dumbfounded at the job ahead. And how this job was absolutely dangerous.

As Marc had been told, there were four strategic men involved. Doctor Townsend was the top man in charge of the Intergalactic Research Society. Doctor Marvin Smyth headed the designing of the new Spaceships. Marc was now studying with Smyth. He also studied with Doctor Jacob March who had the tough job of researching the ramifications of the space equipment and ships. Marc was now learning to be in charge of training the young men who would eventually visit the new planet to assist the new humans who would live there. The fourth man who had been meeting with Marc every day was Father Francis who was to lift Marc's consciousness to the highest spiritual level possible. Of all his mentors, Marc had to admit that he had the greatest need and appreciation for Father Francis Campion.

Each professor had his own genius and Marc had been training with all four of them for eight demanding weeks. Lessons which would have taken four college years had been stuffed into this hard course. But even these short weeks had left his teachers up in arms at not being further along with the project. The horrendous job of turning a small new planet into a home for humans was on a tight time schedule due mainly to the speed of the planet's progress.

THE NEW PLANET

Marc had only one complaint. He had only been able to have a few words with Alana as they passed in the halls. He knew what a difficult job she had been handed. He knew she was capable of doing a great job with the Animal Project, but he also knew how much stress she must be dealing with. But to his surprise, he missed her as she was, a warm and intelligent woman. He had to admit that her physical beauty touched him as much as her spirituality.

"Harrumph! Where are you, Samson? Did you hear what I just said?" Dr. Smyth said. Marc quickly looked up and smiled. "Right with you, Doctor."

The room rang with a loud crashing noise as the narrow-mouthed brown lab bottle that Alana was working with became a pile of useless glass. The quiet laboratory also rang with the loud yelp she let out when the bottle slipped from her fingers onto the pristine floor of the science lab. To the surprise of the other people working near her, she banged her hands on the lab table so hard that it shook. The other workers watched helplessly as their serious, hard-working woman burst into tears.

Olivia had just come into the lab to pick up some lab test materials for Dr. Smyth. She handed her material to an open-mouthed lab tech and ran over to Alana's side.

"Alana, honey. Everything is all right. Come on, we will go to your room where we can have some privacy." Alana sniffed and accepted a tissue from her friend. Then she got up and took Olivia's hand and they left the lab, leaving a bunch of lab rats to figure out what caused this strange outburst.

Fifteen minutes passed before Alana stopped crying. Olivia, having through many emotional Fallouts sat near with her arm around her friend.

There now, that's better. Everything is all right. You just reached the breaking point. It happens to all of us."

Alana blinked. Oh, what have I done? What will those people think of me?

"They will think you are now one of them. They will feel closer to you and that they have found a new friend."

'But I screamed and broke things. It is more likely they will think they have to call out the army."

Olivia laughed. "They have all gone through what you experienced, probably more than once. This work is so intense and so much is counting on it. Institutes like this tend to forget that we are human beings," She tilted Alana's chin up so she could see her eyes. "You will find when you go back to work tomorrow that a lot of that pressing stress will have lessened. From what I hear you are doing a great job in a field totally new to you."

"But I should go back now. There is so much to do." Alana said.

"No darling. You have the rest of the day off. That is, most of it. Father Campion wants to see you for a few minutes. You just take a nice hot shower and put on a pretty dress. He said for you to take your time."

Olivia rose and helped Alana up. Then she gave her best friend a big hug. "I'll see you tomorrow."

"Thank you so much, and I promise to be a normal person by then." Alana smiled.

A half hour later Alana knocked on Father Campion's door. The moment she saw him her heart warmed.

From the first moment she came to the institute and met Father Campion she had felt this same warmth in his presence. He was truly a great healer, and his love kept the many over-stressed employees from getting tired and lonely. She knew his secret and she loved him for it. There was only one thing that healed everyone's problem and that was the glue that held the many universes together. Very simply, it was Love.

Father Campion smiled and gave her a hug. "Sit down, my dear." She did so.

"Now what is the problem?" "It is about time you expressed your feelings about this new job of yours. You have been telling me how grateful you are to have been chosen. Now tell me how you really feel about it."

Alana could not look in his eyes. She looked at her hands which were now red and swollen from chemicals and instruments. After a long moment she lifted her eyes to see a smile filled with complete understanding and love that she trembled. They sat silent for a long time. Finally, Alana reached into her soul and told Father Campion what was really in her heart.

"I loved my old job. I felt I was suited to it and it left me with a good feeling about myself. Then this bombshell hit me. It was like being asked to go so far beyond what I was ready for. On the same day I saw pet animals, living dinosaurs, and a great holy man who ran a conservatory for all of the animals ever created by Power One. Then the same day I came home to find a small pink piglet in my apartment. I admit I love Maxwell, but it has just all happened too fast."

Father Campion sat looking at Alana for a long time. He too had been surprised that such a task was given to one so young. For that moment what was in Alana's heart was in his heart too.

"My dear, Father Francis is what in ancient times we called saints. I am sure he believes that you are a loving person who is also brilliant. He is the one who chose you, Alana. Few of our people are blessed with both. I know how hard it must be for you my dear, but I will be praying for you and I know as you learn more your job will become easier for you and you will see how much health and happiness you will be providing. My prayers are for you, Alana. The moment you realize how much you are helping for so many of Power One's animal children, your job will become much easier.

Alana found as she returned to her job that Father Campion was right. Maxwell was right too. She did now love animals and found joy in helping them.

Surprisingly, she found that she was missing Marc Sampson.

Somehow, he made her feel lighter and she enjoyed what they did together. She realized that she must be careful, or she would get too fond of him. She must not fall in love or she would be in the same uncomfortable situation that poor Olivia was in. She was going to have a baby and was afraid of losing her job.

"Are you being lazy again, Lady?" Marc came up behind her and put his arm around her. She laid back in his arms then realized what she was doing and pulled away. "Hey, no fair. You have a choice to make a man happy or break his heart."

She blushed. "Just being careful, sir. Someone might see us and get the wrong idea." He let her go slowly and his arms felt so wonderful that she blushed again. "You are not afraid of me, are you?" She looked up into his eyes and thought she saw some feelings. It scared her but pleased her more. As her eyes held his, she started trembling. He leaned down and placed his lips on hers and she melted into the kiss. She was almost lost, but she finally pulled away. "We cannot let this happen.". He smiled. "I know. Please stop tempting me."

Alana pushed him away and he smiled. "All right. I will be a good boy, but you tempt me, Lady." She forced a smile on her face. "I will see you later. I'm late for the lab."

As she turned, he slapped her on her behind. She let out a yip and headed for the labs. She knew she was in trouble now for the wonderful feelings she had when he kissed her. She would have to be careful when he was around. But having him close did things to her body. She spoke to herself as she entered the lab, "Give me that lab instrument!"

Marc could have kicked himself. Now he wanted her even more. How in the hell did this happen? He had thought she was a little stuffy at first, but she had become beautiful to him. He had better watch his body or it would really get him in trouble like old Marvin was with Olivia.

He had eight new men in his class on learning to handle the new small spaceships that would carry one man at a time down to the new planet. His classes also delved into the job that each man who landed would have to help the residents. Because of the speed the planet made in growing, there were people already there.

Three weeks later the first trial landing was to take place. Marc had chosen a young man from Trigosa. He was smart and brave. However, he came down with a bad cold and would not be allowed to go down. Marc did not want to change the date as so much hard

THE NEW PLANET

work had been done, but no other student was ready to go down, so he decided to go himself.

"Oh, no. I am in trouble," Alana sighed. "are they out of their minds?" she cried. Marc was too important to let him take a chance like that. Of course, it was none of her business. Or was it?

What if he did not comeback. Oh no! She was in love with him. How could her heart betray her like that? If it had just been her naughty body that needed him. It was her heart, damn it. Olivia had had her son and the child had been taken away and was being raised by one of the ladies who worked in the kitchens. Well, she would pray for Marc and Power One would bring him back to her.

Alana could not help it. She had to see him off. She pushed herself to the front near the small opening in the new small spaceship, and that what it was, not a ship, but was a new small, one-man, self-powered spacesuit. It was small and did not look reliable. Finally, Marc got away from the crowd and pulled her away and into his arms.

"Lady, I don't give a damn what trouble we will be in, I love you." She was ecstatic. "I love you too. Please come back to me." He hugged her, then kissed her deeply. "You know I will. You better wait for me. I do not fall in love every day."

Marc was pulled away from her and secured into the spacesuit. As the crowd watch in awe Marc was slipped into a wormhole and was on his way. Alana held her breath until she choked. He was gone. She might never see him again. How was she going to deal with this? She had always thought she would never fall in love, but she had been wrong, and love was bringing pain instead of happiness. Please, Power One. Please bring him back to me.

Marc could hear the sounds of the air in the wormhole as he tumbled down. He felt no pain as the suit was a fantastic design and supported his body well. He landed much sooner than he expected, and he still felt fine. As he slipped out of the wormhole, he found himself in a range of mountains. No sign of people yet. He slipped out of the spacesuit and hid it behind some smaller boulders. He sat down on a large stone and examined the territory. He took in a big breath. "Wow. They had done it!" This was a real planet with trees and cactus and secure ground. He could not help but be proud of all they had created.

There was little soil for him to hide his spacesuit, so he found a few smaller rocks and put them on top of it. Looking over the terrain he had no idea where a town might be discovered. So, he climbed down the rocks to the ground which he was facing and started walking. About three on his watch time, he finally saw a small man walking toward him. "Are you lookin for Brainstown? I can get you there." Marc waved him toward himself and the little man rushed up to tap him on the arm. "The name is Little. You do not look like you come from here, sir." Marc put out his hand for a handshake but got a puzzled look instead. "Oh, I guess different towns have different ways of saying hello. My Name is Marc Sampson. Please lead me into your city. I am most anxious to see it."

The town was not far, and they reached it in fifteen minutes. Little smiled. "We might have a little trouble in the town because you look so different from all of us. Where did you come from?" "You wouldn't know of it. It is a long way away." When they entered a small town, Marc smiled to see so many healthy-looking people. There had been many tries and the bodies of the people and their ability to do things has by now produced these intelligent looking people. These people were wonderful. But his visit came to a fast stop. Two husky and hairy men grabbed Marc and dragged him into a large building. One big man tried to catch Little, but he yelled at them with "Leave me alone. I am in with the big slob." The man stopped and bowed to Little. The man then indicated that Little and Marc follow him. They did.

They were led into a huge room that was decorated with flowers and pictures of a big fat man in golden robes. Then they were led to a beautiful throne where they were told to kneel before the leader. They did. Shining silver curtains were opened to reveal the leader. He was the fat man in all the pictures. Marc was aghast at the fat bearded leader could actually be a ruler. Then the leader spoke out in an extremely loud and raspy voice.

"Who are you who has interrupted my day. You are quite ugly, and your clothes are a disgrace. Marc looked around to see who the

THE NEW PLANET

leader was yelling at. You the ugly one! Marc could not believe it, but the leader was looking at him. He cleared his throat and spoke. "Sir, I am a visitor at your interesting town, and I am happy to meet its leader." At this point Little grabbed Marc's arm. "OH, I am so sorry that I did not warn you. You are in great trouble now" Marc answered him, "What are you saying? I have done no harm." Before Marc could speak the leader had knocked Little to the ground and called three huge men who picked Marc up from the floor and lifted him up in front of the leader. "I great Buckybundleman' now give you a golden cup." Marc relaxed. you can look at it while you are in our dungeons." Marc grabbed the cup when it was thrown and held onto it while two huge man lifted him and Little up and carried them down dark and cold stairs. They were then thrown into a small cold room. Marc was discouraged that he had not been able to help the towns people, but Little sat smiling. "We have to find a way to get out of here." "It is all right." Marc did not like Little's attitude. Do you want to stay here?" Little smiled. "I do not mind it." Marc gave up. "Where did you get the name 'Little'?" "I guess it was our gallant leader. He claimed he liked me a 'little' so that became my name." Marc tried again. "Let's find a way out of this cell! "It would take a lot of time and we could be beat up. We will be out of here in a couple hours." Marc looked at him," What are you talking about? We could be in here for years and I cannot stay." "Oh no. Buckybundleman always let his prisoners out at ten o'clock in the morning, a half hour from now." "Lets them out. Why put anyone in at all?

"He has to show that he is a great leader. Hey, here they are. We are out and we can go get your suit." Little smiled. "But when we get out, we have to be careful that no one is following us."

"Let us get out of here. We can go around the back and see if we can disappear." Marc said.

They were successful in escaping the dungeon and getting out of town. By the time they reached their destination they were so tired they collapsed on the rocks and fell asleep. Marc woke up first and he dug up his space uniform and checked it out. It did not look too bad. He figured they could get it good enough to take him home to Alana. Then he collapsed on the rocks and slept until late the next morning.

Surprisingly, Little was already up and ready to go to his home to get his tools.

Mark decided to go with him when he said it was only two miles. So off they went. They discussed the equipment and Marc was excited about it. It took them an hour and a half to get there and pick out the tools they would need. When they got there, they were shocked when they found that Little's place had been robbed and torn down. Little fell down on his knees and Marc put his hands over his face. Both were not only shocked but broken hearted. "Oh, how will I make my living." Little cried. Marc added "how will I stay alive?" Both sat on the ground and felt the loss. After a few minutes Little perked up. "My enemy. He did this. I know he did as he has been eyeing my equipment for years. Let us go and get them back. He is only ten miles away and I still have my weapons hidden away." Marc's brain whirled. Another chance to get home to his love. Time was flowing away as he was supposed to be back at the institute in forty more days. He knew he could not make that time, but this might get him home safely with a lot of prayers to Power One.

Marc was terribly disappointed when he saw Little's weapons. Guns were what he had pictured but he realized that he was too far back in time for guns. But the enemy would not have guns either, so he decided to take his or their chances. One thing looked good, there was a supply of food hidden in a tub, so they filled their tummies and took a short nap. When they got up, they picked the most likely weapons and set off with them on their shoulders. Little had been right because they reached the enemies camp in short time. Little told Marc to wait while he checked to see if his enemies were in camp. He was smiling when he returned. "They are not here but my tools are. They must have thought I would not be able to attack them. We must grab the tools and get out of here before they return. They are big strong men, and I am not looking forward to fighting them. Let us hurry." They quickly gathered the pile of tools and set off for Little's place. Marc picked the tools he thought could repair his space suit and they set out for the place his suit was hidden. They were halfway there when they were set upon by two burley men. Little called out "It is them, two of them. You take the tall man."

Marc acted so swiftly that his man fell to the ground unconscious. "I am sure glad I kept up with my fighting lessons." He laughed and took on the second man. Little tripped the man and Marc knocked him out. Little started laughing. "That was fun." Marc smiled. "You bet it was. We are almost to the rocks. Come on." It took two days to repair Marc's space suit, but they were not able to repair the radio without glass parts which were not in Little's tools. Marc rubbed his head. "This is not good. I must notify base that I am ready to start home. They take over from there so they can reverse the wormhole and pull me back." Little looked at Marc closely. "Do you have a woman there?" Marc looked at Little closely. "How did you know?"

"Your urgency. I had a woman once. She was my wife, but our so-called leader took her away from me and she died in his so-called care."

"Oh, I am so sorry. How could you stand to be in his presence?" Marc stopped for a few moments, then continued. "Yes, I am in love with a beautiful woman who blessedly loves me too. She is waiting for me to come back to her and...look where I am."

"She will be praying for you. Whoever your God is, he will be listening."

Alana hesitated before she knocked on Father Campion's door. Everyone knew Marc was dead now. Too much time had passed with no word from him. Finally, she reached up and knocked. The door opened and went in. "Sorry Father. Do you have a few minutes?" Father Campion smiled. "I have all the minutes in the world for you, my dear. Come in, sit down. I have been waiting for you." "Do you think Marc is dead?" He smiled. "No, do you?" Alana sighed. "I keep having these feelings that he is alive and trying to get back to me...us." He sat down next to her. "I have found in my many years that feelings like that are often valid. We have had no proof that Marc is dead, only that he might be. Until we have that proof, we must assume that he is alive somewhere trying to get back to you...us."

"Will you pray with me?" "Of course. May I hold your hands?" She put her hands in his. He prayed silently for a long time, then asked Alana to say her own prayers, which she did. "Power One, I thank you for all of your blessings. I love you and I love Marc Sampson. You know where he is, so I ask you to take care of him and bring him back to me.

Thank you for providing him with whatever he needs to find the reverse wormhole we are sending to the new planet so he can return home to we who love him. Thank you with all my heart."

"Well then, that should do it, my dear. Let me know when you have evidence that Marc has found the worm hole and is on his way home." She smiled. "Yes, Father. You will be the first to know. Thank you so much from my heart to yours." She went to work with a lighter heart that morning. She had promised Olivia that she would look in on her son in a small apartment where Olivia had a chance to visit him. He was a fine little boy and was always happy and loved to visit with his parents and Alana when they could find the time. However, now that Olivia and Martin were married, she was with child again. Olivia loved Alana and she was praying for Marc too. Olivia's prayers were that Marc was alive, Alana's were for Marc to find a way home to her. Every day at work seemed like a year. She questioned all the employees to see if anyone had a way for Marc to get home, but they would look at her and sigh. They knew he must be dead.

Then came the biggest request from Alana that they could not even believe. She wanted to go down to the planet to find Marc and bring him home. This request was pushed away from every one of the leaders as total fantasy, but Alana argued with each Doctor in charge until they set up a hearing with the whole lot of them.

The bosses were sure they could talk her out of this foolish idea, but she surprised them with a total plan for her trip that they were amazed and found it hard to say no to.

The units that would be called upon to set this plan up were flabbergasted. Their answers to putting this plan in order started with 'they were too busy' and went on to 'the woman is crazy'. But Alana would not be stopped. She joined every unit and led them each into the safest way for her to follow in Marc's trail. When each unit studied Alana's plans, they had to admit that she had a strong case.

They finally became excited about it. Sending a woman to the new planet made some sort of sense as she could work on her animal study if she could not find Sampson. They were all ready to do an exciting landing, so the bosses finally gave in. Alana was scheduled to leave one week from the day, and everyone was working especially hard to keep this brave woman alive.

Alana had to admit that she was scared to death of going down a worm hole to the strange planet below. However, she loved Marc and if there was any chance, he was alive and she could find him… well, she had to go!

Every unit worked their heads off to meet the date of Alana's departure, especially the unit that had to expand the room in the wormhole so that two people could return in it the same time.

Alana was everywhere giving advice and churning up arguments. Despite this everything was ready on the appropriate day.

Father Campion was the last to say goodbye to Alana. He held her hands and prayed with her for both to come safely home. Knowing how far she would have to travel in the cold wormhole set her to shivering, but she kept saying Marc's name and she had a safe landing on the new planet.

She realized that there were sounds of people. She was frightened but if there was a town, Marc might be there. She walked slowly towards the sounds and soon found herself in a small town with people in bright colors. One woman approached her. "We must get you a dress. Our leader would not like to see you dressed like a man." Alana started to turn away, but a group of women joined the woman who had approached her first. They grabbed her and dragged her to a booth where many colorful dresses hung.

"How do you speak English?" One woman yelled to her, "Our great leader has a box a young man left with him. It taught us how to talk like he did."

Alana's heart pumped louder. "A young man. Do you know his name?" Another woman answered, "No, but our great leader knows. Come we must dress you up. You cannot stand in front of him dressed like that." At this juncture, Alana let them dress her in an incredibly beautiful and sexy dress, in case their leader might know where Marc was. Maybe he was here. Her heart thumped.

One woman took he hand and led her to a large building. They entered and were led to a huge room which surprised Alana by its richness and beautiful colored drapes. The woman took Alana before the throne and pushed her down on the floor. She wanted to get up but finally decided she had better stay where she was.

She jumped when some loud bells rang and a fat man in colorful draped clothing appeared and took the throne. She tried to examine him, but she got caught looking up and a gong rang out. The fat man spoke loudly. "You dare to look at the leader before you are allowed to?" Alana figured she better not talk. His loud voice rang out. "Much better. You may tell me who you are and what you are doing in my town."

Alana watched this monster for a few more seconds. Then she spoke, "May I stand in your great presence?" This leader thought for a few minutes, then smiled showing no teeth. "A good idea. I want to see you better." At the sound of his voice Alana turned and tried to run. She was stopped by two strong women and the wrap over the dress was quickly visible. The leader laughed, a horrid sound. Alana tried to get away, but her legs were held to the floor. She was so embarrassed. She quickly covered the visible tops of her breasts. Then she heard words that would ruin her search for Marc.

"She is a treasure. Ladies make the wedding as fast as you can. She is a treasure and I want her for my own. He laughed out loud and ordered some chimes as he watched Alana fall to the floor in a deep faint. He laughed again, louder. "Ladies take her to my rooms and wake her up. I have lots of questions to ask, Move!"

When Alana woke up, she found herself in a huge and beautiful bed and she was nude. She quickly got up and wrapped a sheet around her. She looked around the room to find a place she could get out. She ran to a doorway that looked good but was met by two

THE NEW PLANET

soldiers. She smiled at them and backed away. "Just need to relieve my bladder, sirs." "You will find a kettle under your bed." Suddenly she had a thought. "Say how is it that you can speak my language? One of the soldiers smiled. Young man came here and gave the leader a box. It held the secret of the way he spoke. But you also talk like this." "Oh, my God! Did the man have curly blond hair? Please say YES.

You talk to our leader He will be right in. He was right. When the leader entered the two soldiers bowed on their knees then left the room. Alana was frightened now. She could not stay with this monster. Now that she knew Marc was alive, she had to escape. For now, she had to think of some way to keep him from raping her. He stood in all his spender, his toothless mouth hanging open. She spoke. "The man who came from afar place and gave you the box that lets you understand us. Where is he?"

The leader was surprised and moved back. "He was my friend. He survived my dungeons. Why do you ask about him?" Alana found her way. She looked straight into the leader's eyes and said "He is my husband and I want to take him home.

"Your husband! Do not say that. I cannot marry a woman who is married. What am I to do with you?" Alana looked him straight in the eye, because only one of his eyes were open. "His name is Marc Sampson, and he is a leader on our home planet. I think he might be injured so I must find him."

The leader sat down on his huge bed and looked sad. "I should have kept him here. I liked him. He survived my deepest dungeons and gave me back my golden cup. Oh, if we can find where Little lives, he might be with him. They came here together.

Alana jumped up. 'Can we go now. We can take some of your soldiers with us'.

"Surly. But you have seen my soldiers. I only have two. Is that all right?" Alana jumped up. Her heart pounding. "I will need my clothes. We might have to fight, and this dress was not made for fighting." The leader signaled a woman to bring the clothes, but the woman shook her head. "She should not change here. I will get her into her clothes and bring her back to you."

He nodded. Twenty minutes later Alana was dressed and ready to go. "Where are your soldiers?"

He pulled a strange horn from his shirt and blew on it. The two soldiers appeared immediately and bowed before their leader. "You are fine men and I need you to go with this woman and help her find the nice young man you admired so much. She is his wife."

One of the men asked, "Will we need weapons?" The leader nodded. The men looked at Alana. "Oh, it is you. We will be glad to protect you Miss." "It is Mrs, and we are going to find my husband. Where do you think we should start?" One of the soldiers had a blank face but the other one had an idea. "He was the blond man from another world was he not?" Alana perked up. "Yes, yes!

Do you remember him?" "Yes, I do. We saw him a few times with a small man named Little."

"Do you know where this man lives?" We have been there several times when our leader wanted to see him. If you are ready, we will take you there. Alana was now excited, and they set out for a long walk to the place Little lived. But when they got there all they found was a broken-down shelter and quite a mess. The soldiers were sad that Mr. Little was not there and there was no way to know where he was.

Alana fought to hold back tears of disappointment.

"It is obvious that he has been attacked by his enemies. Would you have any idea who they might be?" The obviously brighter soldier spoke up. "There are a group of rough criminals not far from here. Do you wish to go there Mrs.?

Alana knew she did not have a choice. She had to find Marc as soon as she could.

"I am ready. Let us try at Mr. Little's enemies' place. They might still be there." So, they set off. It only took one hour to reach the place and they were then told by a friend of Littles that Little had gone with his friend up to the rock mountains.

Alana checked with the bright soldier and he said he knew where the rock mountains were, and he would be glad to take her there. "But my soldier friend is not feeling well. He is not used to so much action. Can we send him home?" Alana smiled. "Of course.

THE NEW PLANET

Does he know the way?" "He has a paper in his pocket that will show him the way. If he does not follow it, I will find him later and take him home." Alana watched the soldier go and tapped the strong soldier on the shoulder. "We can go now, can we not?" He smiled. "You are kind so we will now be on our way to the Rock Mountains. They travelled quickly and by noon they reached their destination.

When the got there the soldier said 'It will be hard going when we get into those big rocks. Do you want to go on?" "Of course," Alana smiled.

So, they started to climb but before they got very far a loud bang sounded. The soldier backed up. "It sounds like a weapon we do not have. "Oh, my lord. It sounded like a gun. Do you have guns?" "No. Do not know what they are." "Do not move. I am going in." The soldier was shocked. "I cannot let you go into danger without me at your side." "It is…It might be my husband. He has a gun. He will not hurt me." All right, but I will follow at a distance." Alana crawled over the smaller rocks and kept popping her head up to look ahead. She tripped and made a noise, and another shot rang out. She stopped and yelled out, "Marc. Marc is that you?" She screamed when she heard Marc's voice. "Marc it is me, it is Alana!" "Do you think I am a fool? Alana is home safe." "No Marc, it's me, Alana. I came here to find you." Marc answered, I cannot believe that, but you do sound like Alana. Who are you?" I am Alana, darling. I came to find you. It is me. Then Alana heard a tumble of stoned and Marc fell into her arms.

"Oh, my lord! It is you. What the hell are you doing here. I thought you were safe at home." "And I thought a kiss would be more appropriate." Alana answered. Marc stared at her for a moment then pulled her to him and kissed her thoroughly.

"What the hell are you doing here?" Marc questioned. "Everyone said you were dead, but I did not believe you were. I would have known." "But why did they let you come. We might never get back home." "Is there anything left of your ship?" "Yes, Little and I have fixed it up. All we need is a…" "A worm hole protector, of course." Alana smiled. "You have one?" Marc shouted. "I would not come down here without a way for two people to return." Marc kept "his arms around Alana. "We better get going. Little, I am going to miss you." Little gasped "Oh am I not going with you?" Alana and Marc both looked at him. They were both surprised. Marc patted Little on the back

"Do you not want to stay on your own planet?"

What did you say? What is a planet?" Marc answered. 'Sorry, it is a big round solid and, well it holds life of every type. People live on this round piece of land and water…like we are doing now. It is where we all live on. This planet that we are standing on now is your home. We live on a different planet that is quite different." Little smiled "Then I want to go to your planet with you."

Marc looked at Alana. She took over. "I am so sorry, but our planet has air that is heavier. You would not be able to breath." Little tried again to keep his friends. "Then can you stay here a little longer?" Marc looked to Alana. She took a long time to answer.

"Marc, I have been thinking. There are no animals here. I would like to find out where they, and if they, are doing well. It would not hurt if we stayed a little longer. I can notify my unit that it is part of my job and we want to stay here at least a week." Marc looked unhappy. "I have been dreaming about going home. He let go of his sad look and smiled. "But I have you with me now and anywhere is heaven. I say a month might give us time with whatever animals we can locate. We can stay here…together." Alana was happy now. She ran into his arms and was rewarded with a big hug and a fantastic kiss.

Little was jumping up and down and yipping. When he stopped, he had good news, "You two can stay at the home tent of my friends. They will love to meet you and you will be safe. I am going to my home to repair it. I must dig a basement to keep my tools safe. Then I will join you in your hunt for…what did you call them?" Marc was shocked. "You have never seen an animal?" Little replied "How could I know. I may have seen them, but I would have had no way of knowing they were animals." Alana laughed. "Now there is a smart man. Marc smiled. "It is still early. We can go to out temporary home and then start on out quest." He turned to Alana. "Have you told our unit that we are staying for a while to find some animals?" She gave him a quick kiss on his cheek. "Everything has been approved. They just want us to notify them if we run into danger. I promised. So, we can leave now." Marc replied. "Cannot leave until Little finished a cart to carry the suits." Alana pouted. "Do we have to drag them along?" Marc looked surprised. "We do not know where we might be forced to put them on and call for help."

She smiled. "Of course. Oh, darling I am so glad you agreed to stay here a little longer. I am so excited that we might find some of the animals I sent down.

When they arrived at the home of Little's friends' home, they were surprised to see a huge tent made of all different colored fabric. Marc tested the material and was amazed to see how smooth and strong it was. Two young people rushed out to meet them. The girl was in the family way and she was quite pretty. The man was tall, and he had a fully muscled body. Both were smiling and held their hands out to Alana and Marc. The woman spoke but Marc could not understand her. He looked at Alana. She returned his look and confessed. "Oh well I do not feel so guilty now." Marc looked confused. She continued. "When I was trapped in the Leader's room, I stuffed the language box under my jacket." Marc was confused. "You were at that awful place?" Alana smiled. "Oh yes. I almost became the leader's wife." Marc was upset now. "My lord. How did you get out of that?"

She smiled again. "I told him we were married." Marc laughed. "Good girl. And in spite of orders at the institute you will be as soon as we get home." Alana was surprised. "Are my ears working or are you asking me to marry you?" "Damned right. Are you going to say yes so we can use the language box and can talk to these nice people?" Alana was in heaven. She had prayed for this for years and had almost given up. She threw her arms around Marc and kissed him. "Damned right I am going to say yes. YES! Marc kissed her back and they stood hugging for a long time. Alana finally spoke. "Do you have any idea how much I love you?" Marc smiled. "Oh sure. About fifty percent of how I love you." Alana moved into Marc's arms. "I can think of something more fun than arguing." "Then follow me into our rented room. There is much I have not taught you yet."

"I am at your heels, darling man."

The next morning the pair were full of smiles and sweet words. Little was touched because he could still remember life with his pretty wife. When breakfast was over Little questioned Alana and Marc. "Have you two decided where you are going next?"

Marc looked at Alana. "It is up to my wife. She has a job she wants to do." Alana smiled. "Yes, we will be headed out for the wild land to see what we find there."

Little spoke. "Are you aware that there is another city about five hundred miles in front of you?"

Alana looked surprised. "No, I did not know that. I hope they are not like the one near here." Little answered her. "Thank goodness, it is a wonderful and beautiful city, much bigger than this one. You will like it. They speak my language. Before Marc used his box on me." Alana spoke up. "Well, we will go there only if we have to. The animals are most important." Marc put his arm around Alana. "We better get going before it gets hot." Alana agreed and they said thank you and goodbye to their hosts. "Goodbye. Little. You have been a good friend." Marc said. Little jumped up and down. "But I am going with you." Alana spoke. "We love you dear Little but we cannot ask you to leave your home and go with us on this search. It could get dangerous."

"My home no longer exists, and you are my best friends. Please let me go with you." Marc looked at Alana. "Honey?" "Well, he might find a new home in this fancy city." "Ah ha! My thoughts as well. Get your things together, Little. Here we go."

It did not take them long to reach the big city. It was uniquely beautiful with colorful flowering plants everywhere. What thrilled Alana was the sounds of barking. As they walked through the huge gateway a large dog came running toward them barking angrily. When he saw Alana, he stopped. He moved toward her slowly. Alana was not afraid of him, so she offered him her hands. The dog moved close to her his tail now wagging. Alana kneeled and greeted him with her arms. They both were obviously happy.

Little and Mark both took in a large breath, now able to breathe again, Marc leaned over and dropped one pat on the dog's head.

THE NEW PLANET

He looked at Alana and shook his head. "How did you know?" She smiled. "I knew he was one of ours because I knew that these people would not have any animals until I sent them down. He had to be ours." The dog stayed at Alana's side as they entered the town or seeing it now it should probably be called a city. Shortly a woman greeted them, but she spoke a different language. Marc complained. "Oh, I left the machine in that old town." Alana smiled.

"No problem. I have the latest version. It is small enough to fit in my pocket. Marc reached for it and Alana pulled it from her pocket and gave it to him.

The woman who was waiting patiently spoke to them again in her own language. Marc smiled at her and took her hand, "We will fix this right now." He looked closer at the equipment and turned to Alana again. Marc gave her a puzzled look. "All right, how do you work this thing? Alana held the unit in her hands as she instructed Marc. "It is easy, see. Just one twist and you put the instrument on to the person's forehead." Marc took one more look at the small unit and reached out to touch the woman's forehead. She pulled away and screamed. "Oh, I am sorry. It is all right I mean no harm." The woman looked at him. "Damn, she does not understand. You do it." Alana smiled as she comforted the woman and touched her forehead with the language instrument, this time she was not afraid and smiled. Alana spoke softly. "Do you understand me?" The woman had a shocked look on her face. How can this be? I only know one language so, how can I understand you? Marc looked at Alana so, she explained to the woman who finally walked away with a question still on her mind. Alana complained. "Oh, we should have asked her where the office of their leader is." Marc comforted her. "I am sure we can find it if we walk toward the middle of the city. It is a wonderful place and I bet they have a few good restaurants." Alana smiled "Thanks for reminding me of my empty stomach. To heck with the leader. Let us find some food right now." All three agreed and they soon found a place to eat and had a happy lunch. After their tummies were full, they felt so much better that they decided to tour the city before they looked for the leader.

Both were excited at the buildings and homes. They were far more modern than they should be. The dog was following Alana's every step. After blocks and blocks were studied Marc said they should now find the leader, Alana agreed so they started to look at the middle of town. Suddenly the woman they had spoken to earlier ran up to them. "Oh, how I have searched for you." Alana took the woman's hands in hers. "Why whatever is the problem." "I am the only person in the city who does not speak like anyone else. I want my languish back, please." Alana calmed her. "Please do not worry. Soon everyone will speak in ours and your language. The woman was confused, "But, how can that be?" Marc was getting very tired of the delays. We are taking care of that. Please try to be patient." The woman turned her nose up at Marc and walked away. Alana looked at Marc. "We better find the leader before we turn the whole town against us." He huffed. "You are right. Let us find the leader."

"He must be very rich" Alana noted. Marc grabbed her hand and started walking. She smiled and quickened her steps. It did not take long to find the beautiful, gilded building that housed the leader. They were met by a tall man of about fifty. He bowed and introduced himself to be Honorable House Master. Marc told him who they were and that they wished to meet their leader. The House Master smiled. "He will be happy to meet you. He works very hard. Please follow me."

They followed him to a huge, guilded room which was decorated with bright golden walls. Alana took a fast breath and whispered to Marc. "This is fantastic. We do not have anything like this on our planet. It is hard to believe." They did not have to wait too long. There was a gorgeous throne which was slightly hidden. They could see the figure of a man. When The leader's face was revealed. Alana let out a scream. Marc was suddenly joyful. "Martin! It is you! How did this happen?" Martin jumped up, leaped off the throne and grabbed Marc in a strong hug. "My Lord. How are you two here?" Marc laughed. "Get down off that throne and we can talk. And talk they did. It did not take too long for Marc and Alana to tell their stories and Martin was thrilled to have them on his planet. His story sounded a little like theirs.

THE NEW PLANET

Olivia had urged Martin to find out what happened to Marc and Alana. He had believed that it was a bad idea and argued that Marc and Alana tried going down and where were they. But Olivia cried every night, so he finally made the trip down to the little planet. When he found this beautiful city, he had been surrounded. The people thought he was a God down from heaven. He had tried to tell them he was not a god, but they could not understand what he was saying so they built this building for him and placed him on a throne. He had finally decided to learn their language and be a good leader and take care of them. His only complaint was that he did not have Olivia and his children.

Then it was Marc's turn. He told Martin what had happened to Alana and him and what he and Alana were up to. The party were led into another large room where lovely tables topped with beautiful tablecloths and many large flowers in shiny holders.

They were up late talking. They were so happy to be together. The next morning, they had a big breakfast. Alana kept smiling but she was disappointed that the city held no dogs.

Martin smiled. "Do come with me, Alana. I have a present for you." Alana was curious so, she followed Martin to a large outdoor area behind the building. Alana was joyful when she saw what Martin was talking about. It was in a nice outside garden area. And there were at least five mother dogs and many puppies of different breeds. She let out a happy scream and many Thank You's to Martin. "Oh, Martin. Thank you so very much. I was beginning to think that none of my animals survived." walked over and put his arm around Alana. "I am glad you are pleased. There are many wild ones out in the hills." Alana was so happy. "But I know you cannot be so happy without your wife and your children."

I have been offered many young women, but I still love Olivia. These people are so sure that I am their God that I feel guilty when I want to get home. Alana leaned in to him. "I know how you must feel Martin, but you are not their God. You are not truly able to help them. They are new people on a new planet, and they will have to learn what is good for themselves." Martin went into deep thought. After a moment he smiled wide at Alana. "You are right, Alana." I have waited for over a year to make me feel I am doing the right thing. My people will be very unhappy though." Marc joined Martin and Alana. "Sorry but I have been listening. I have an idea that might help.

Martin sat down and listened to Marc's idea.

That night an announcement was made over the city and to people outside the gates.

All were shocked and some said that they would kill themselves. All people who believed in their Power One should be at the throne that evening at midnight in the Thone Room to see their own Power One off to rise into the clouds to receive his rewards. It worked! Of course, the Throne Room was way over-crowded, so the streets were filled with mournful people. Marc and Little had made a giant sign with angels on it and people crowded around to say goodbye and send love to their Power One. Everyone was sad, but they seemed to have their renewed and their faith and sent Martin off with much faith that he would guard them from above.

Meanwhile, Martin, Marc, Alana, and Little were on their way to the mountains where Marc had left his spacesuit and Alana's. It was a long way back and Marc wanted to bypass the small town that was ruled by The Leader. Now they were all ready to go home, but one person was not entirely happy. Alana wanted so to see some of the animals that were out in the hills.

They stopped and sat around a warm fire and ate some of the food Marc had saved.

Marc put his arm around Alana and kissed her. "Look honey, we can see them when we fly over. I think we need to check in at home. We can get Martin home and visit Olivia and get some rest." Alana looked over the suits and was about to agree but let out a yip. "Oh, my Lord. How did this happen. These suits are a mess. How could this have happened?"

Little tried to hide his guilty face, but Alana spotted it as Little turned to leave. She shouted "Little." Little turned around. "I am so sorry Alana. I just could not see that you and Marc would go and leave me behind. I will fix them for you. I know how and I will do a good job." "It is all right, Little. I will help you. They settled down to work and in four hours the suits were as good as new. Alana turned to Little. "Maybe we can take you up later. We will be working here on and off. You are our friend, Little. We will not desert you."

Marc joined them. "I am trying to figure out should we take Martin back or should we bring Olivia and the two children down here. Martin is doing pretty well for himself." Marc thought for a moment. "Well, Olivia was never in love with her job like we were. I'll give her a call when Little has finished the communicator." "I want to speak to her too. And tell her how fashionable Martin's palace is." Marc laughed. "You women sure like your luxuries." Alana poked Marc. "You are my only luxury." Marc answered, "Funny I thought you were my luxury. They laughed and settled the argument with a kiss.

The next morning found Marc and Alana on home ground. The first person Alana went to see was Father Campion. She was full of thanks for their safe arrival and wanted to thank him for his prayers for them while they were on the new planet. Then she had a job to take care of with Olivia. How was she going to explain the problem to Olivia? Letting her know her husband was a king in a palace on a new planet was not exactly easy to believe.
So, she talked Father Campion to go to Olivia with her. Alana told Olivia a little about the new planet and then told her where they had found Martin. Olivia yipped. "Oh, how stupid I am. I forgot to tell you that he had gone missing. I have been worrying for weeks."

"Well, your worries are over. Your loving husband is on the New Planet." Olivia dropped what she was doing and grabbed Alana's hands. "Oh, dear. Is he all right?" "He is more than all right. He is King and has a palace to live in." Olivia dropped into a chair. Alana put her arms around her friend. "I know he will want you and the children to come down. He just wanted you safe in your journey down." Olivia jumped up. "You do not know Martin do you? Oh, we are going down there, whether he wants us or not!

Father Campion addressed Olivia. "Mrs., I hope you will go down there with love and forgiveness in your heart." Olivia smiled. "Oh, I will forgive him when I am the queen."

Alana turned her face away to hide her smile, but when she looked at him, he was smiling too. Alana and Olivia and of course the two children left for the New planet the next day. It was a big package to send but the senders were good at what they did, and all felt safe. They landed outside of Martin's city and all were glad to be on solid ground at last. Olivia looked and looked but did not see Martin here to greet them. She started to scream, but Alana silenced her. "Wait Olivia. I did not tell him we were coming. I wanted it to be a surprise." But mainly because she wanted to see Martin's face when they appeared.

Marc laughed way out loud when he learned Olivia and the children were here. "I will not let you go unless I am there too." "Sure, we want you there. Olivia is changing into her best dress and the children are changing, too." Marc tuned in too. "Good and we all need a good laugh. Let us go, here they are" They all walked fast and rushed into the large room of the castle and ran in front of the throne. Martin was sitting on the throne but was turned around facing the back of the throne. When a loud bell rang, he turned around and saw his family. "This is going to be fun." But, when Martin turned around and saw his family, he jumped off the throne and grabbed Olivia and the children in his arms, hugging and kissing them. Not too funny. But the laughers were so happy to see the family come together in love that they also hugged and kissed the whole family. The next time Alana saw Olivia she was sitting next to Martin on the wide throne. She was dressed in a beautiful pink gown of satin and lace and the wonderful color was perfect for Olivia. She was beautiful in every way and her smile pleased Alana and Marc tremendously. So, later they got to talk and were surprised that both Olivia and Martin were so happy and that they decided to stay on the New Planet.

THE NEW PLANET

Alana was surprised when Marc wanted to talk so seriously that night. "What is it? I thought everything was all right." "That is what I want to talk about-US." Alana was surprised as their romance had taken second place to the new planet lately. She thought for a moment then spoke. "Sure honey. We have not been too close lately."

Well honey, think I can make a big change in this. This is a pretty nice new planet, is it not?" Alana answered. What I have seen of it I think it will grow into a nice place to live." Marc did not like that answer. "But lots of people are already living on this new planet, as well as Little and Martin and his family. They all seem to be happy." "Oh, I think they have a good thing here. They are starting a new world which shall be an honest try to make a new home for many people, including the ones who will be born here." Marc smiled "And they have no problem with two people getting married either." Alana looked up at him. "Oh, I noticed that, too." "Did you. Well then you should not be surprised when you learn that I have opened a voice to Father Campion at our old home, and he will be marrying us at eight o'clock tonight. "

Oh Marc, do you mean it?" "I would not be saying it if I did not mean it with all my heart. There could not be another woman like you in two planets. I love you so much and I am dying to have a ring on my finger." Alana looked curious. "A ring? What is that about?" Marc smiled. Just because I have a gorgeous ring that belonged to my mother. I think it would look beautiful on you." Alana hugged him "I love it and will be honored to wear it. Thank you sweety."

When they told Martin, they were getting married they got a loud hurray. "It is about time! I am arranging the wedding for you because I love you two crazy people. It will take place tomorrow and will be wonderful. I will bring Father Francis over to this planet and he will give you two his blessings.

Martin was true to his word. The wedding was beautiful except for Alana. She could not stop crying happy tears. But Marc was supremely happy. The gown Martin gave Alana was gorgeous, and in spite of her tears Alana was beautiful too. Marc was finally able to get his wife alone for a moment. "How about it honey. Are we going back to work or are we staying here?" Alana thought for a moment, then asked Marc what he wanted to do. "You know, I am getting fond of this place." Just then Martin joined them. "Hey, you two lovers, I have found the perfect house for you. It is large and lovely. I am sure you will love it." Marc tried to say they we not sure, but it came out "Thank you, friend. We will love it." Alana started laughing and all of them joined her. Alana smiled. "Well, I guess that does it. We are staying on the new planet." And Alana, my gift to you is any fine dog in my kennels." "Oh, thank you so much. Can I go there now?" Martin nodded and Alana ran to the kennels. "Oh, my wonderful animals. I want this one. Thus, there came a happy woman and a happy dog. Marc smiled. "Hey, we keep calling this place the new planet. Does it not have a name of its own?" Alana smiled. "Of course, it does. We are calling it EARTH for our planet restoration project titled: "**E**nvironmental **A**nimation and **R**econstruction of **T**raditional **H**abitats"

www.ingramcontent.com/pod-product-compliance
Lightning Source LLC
LaVergne TN
LVHW021737060526
838200LV00052B/3332